DORA the EXPLORER®

Dora's Perfect Pumpkin

by Kirsten Larsen
illustrated by Victoria Miller

Ready-to-Read

Simon Spotlight/Nick Jr.
New York   London   Toronto   Sydney

Based on the TV series *Dora the Explorer*® as seen on Nick Jr.®

SIMON SPOTLIGHT
An imprint of Simon & Schuster Children's Publishing Division
1230 Avenue of the Americas, New York, New York 10020
Manufactured in the United States of America
First Edition
2 4 6 8 10 9 7 5 3 1
Library of Congress Cataloging-in-Publication Data
Larsen, Kirsten.
Dora's perfect pumpkin / by Kirsten Larsen ; illustrated by Victoria Miller. — 1st ed.
p. cm. — (Ready-to-read ; 14)
"Based on the TV series Dora the Explorer as seen on Nick Jr." —T.p. verso.
ISBN-13: 978-1-4169-3438-7
ISBN-10: 1-4169-3438-3
I. Miller, Victoria, ill. II. Dora the explorer (Television program) III. Title.
PZ7.L323817Dor 2007
2006023075

Hi! I am .
DORA

 is making a  —a  .
ABUELA   PIE   PUMPKIN PIE

Do you like ? I do!
PIE

BOOTS and I have to go

to the PUMPKIN patch.

We will get a PUMPKIN

to make the PIE.

MAP says we need to go

over TROLL BRIDGE

and to the FARM.

We can take this WAGON

to carry our PUMPKIN.

Here is .
TROLL BRIDGE

And here is the .
GRUMPY OLD TROLL

The  has a riddle
GRUMPY OLD TROLL

for us.

"There are **4** seasons.
FOUR

Do you know them all?

They are  , ,
WINTER   SPRING

, and _____."
SUMMER

Do you know the answer?

Right! The answer is "fall."

Good job!

Now we can cross .

TROLL BRIDGE

We made it to the  🏚️.
FARM

We need to find the 🟧.
ORANGE

🎃.
PUMPKINS

Do you see the 🎃 patch?
PUMPKIN

Is this the patch?
PUMPKIN

No. These are not .
PUMPKINS

These are .
TOMATOES

Is this the  patch?
PUMPKIN

No. These are not .
PUMPKINS

These are .
PEPPERS

Is this the patch?
PUMPKIN

Yes!

Look at all the !
PUMPKINS

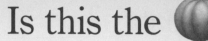

BOOTS and I need to pick a

 PUMPKIN now.

Should we pick this PUMPKIN?

No. It is too big.

Should we pick this 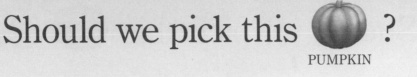 ?

PUMPKIN

No. It is too small.

Should we pick this  ?
PUMPKIN

Yes!

It is the perfect
PUMPKIN

for 's .
ABUELA   PIE

Now we can put the  PUMPKIN

in our WAGON.

We will take it to ABUELA.

We made it!

Now  can make her .

ABUELA

PUMPKIN PIE

 and I help.

We scoop out the

seeds.

Then  mixes ,
ABUELA   SUGAR

, , ,
MILK   EGGS   FLOUR

, and .
CINNAMON   PUMPKIN

The  is done.
PIE

Yum!

It is a perfect 🎃 🥧.
PUMPKIN PIE

Thank you for helping us

today!

She pours it in the .
CRUST

Then she puts it in the .
OVEN

Soon the  will be done.
PIE

The  will taste so good!
PIE